CW00429676

T.M. Cooks is the pen name laborative writing team. The

- Carmen Margaret McAdam

- Denver Mackinlay

- Jaydn Cormack

- Jenna Mackenzie

- Joshua De Oliveira

- Kyle Glatley

- L. Wilson

- Lucy S. Hamilton

with cover design by Joe Reddington. The project was led by:

- Ashley Waner

- Luisa Balewski

The group cheerfully acknowledges the wonderful help given by:

- Kaitlin Sferrazzo

And a big thank you goes to Scottish Government School Library Improvement Fund who funded this wonderful project. Its been a wonderful opportunity, and everyone involved has been filled with incredible knowledge and enthusiasm. Finally, we would like to thank all the staff at Knightswood Secondary School for their support in releasing our novelists from lessons for a full week.

The group started to plan out their novel at 9.00am on Monday 4th September 2023 and completed their last proof reading at 12:30pm on Friday 8th September 2023.

We are incredibly proud to state that every word of the story, every idea, every chapter and yes, every mistake, is entirely their own work. No teachers, parents or other students touched a single key during this process, and we would ask readers to keep this in mind. We are sure you will agree that this is an incredible achievement. It has been a true delight and privilege to see this

group of young people turn into professional novelists in front of our very eyes.

The Flames of Deceit

T. M. Cooks

0

Contents

1

Chapter 1

Freedom on Fire

As she stood on the old, rickety and fragile
bridge that linked the houses of the village to the

market, she stood there in total shock. She could not believe nor fully process what she was witnessing. She wanted to let the screams out, she wanted to let the emotions out, but she couldn't. She froze in fear. Amelia stood perfectly still, in complete silence as she watched a collage of rouge and bright orange flames swallow the old grey castle of Lazurite. It was almost beautiful, a work of art in a way.

However, this would be devastating, a catastrophe, as the flames did not just claim a portion of the castle of Lazurite, it also claimed a very crucial group of people. Not just any ordinary group of people, the group of people inside these flames were the most crucial and important people to the village, they were none other than the kingdom's beloved royal family. The foundation of this kingdom had been swallowed so suddenly by a somewhat breathtaking exhibit. It felt surreal, it felt like it should never have occurred, it felt like a nightmare had come alive.

Amelia felt a certain degree of denial and disbelief as she tried to tell herself that this had never happened when it visibly did. She made her best attempt to process the event that she had just witnessed, she had so many questions that would most likely remain unanswered. She had asked herself, "Who would have done such a thing?" "What did the royals ever do to deserve this?" "Was this intentional or was it simply an act of misfortune that led to the catastrophic death of such a great family?" "Did it even happen¿' Because at this moment it certainly felt dreamlike. She had so many questions with many more to come after. However, one question she could answer was that she was certain of, is that their successor would not be able to fill in their shoes, no one could.

If she was perfectly frank with herself, she just couldn't imagine a kingdom without them. She had no way of seeing any potential for a thriving community after this complete disaster spectacle, that had unfolded right in front of her hazel eyes. In the coming days, the royal successor would be announced and Amelia was certain that she felt uncertain about a whole new era that was about to commence for the village. The royals were the only leaders that Amelia had ever known in the short-lived period of 16 years of her life. To Amelia, it felt like the royals were almost immortal. That obviously was not to be the case as they had been swallowed in a fiery wave of destruction. It was clear, however, that the new leader would impose their way of thinking. Things would be different and it was still a blurry vision as to if that would be a good or a bad thing for the life of the village and its people.

Rumors had spread that the new leader was to be a king. A king with no queen, a king who stood by himself, a king who would have his own morals and his own way of ruling. However it might not be as bad as first thought, as he had been suspected to have known the royal family and if Amelia knew the royals as well as she did, she was assured and convinced that they would have appointed someone who loved and cared for

their people when their time came. Although no
one quite expected the royals to go and for it to
happen so suddenly. However, it had happened
and a new ruler would be in place.

Chapter 2

Ian's Fate

While boiling some water on the stove to make tea, Ian said with a sigh, "The Royal family are gone, What will our village do now?" Victoria reassured Ian with a hand on his heart. "We will do what we have always done, be good neighbours and work hard." The sun was already beating in the morning sky, Ian went on his way to start the day knowing that Victoria was right. While he was plowing his crops and collecting the apples from the apple tree, Ian felt a sense of purpose again after a disastrous few days. He remembered his role here and he refused to let anyone down.

Over the following days, the villagers worried about the rumors of a new leader. The royal family had always supported their village and people. They prayed the new leader would do so too. You would have been able to smell the smoldering smoke in the distance where the castle once stood, which also made the villagers uneasy.

At dawn the next morning, the village bells chimed. A voice from afar called everyone to meet. "I am your new leader, " explained the man. "I have come to take governance over your village." The man stood tall, towering over the villagers that had never looked so small. "We will call into your farms and strike up our deals. Don't disobey or there will be consequences!" he exclaimed.

Suddenly, the prices of items started changing. Farmers had to give around sixty-five percent of their crops to the leader so they were left with a choice of either selling the little they had left to make money or to have food on the table. The villagers were also very restricted on what they could and couldn't do. Instead of being good neighbours and sharing wealth, crops were sold back to the farmers by the new leader.

"Do you remember life before this¿' Ian asked Victoria, his wife. "Yes! we felt free, now I feel trapped and it almost feels like we're prisoners in our own home, " she replied, tearfully.

Ian was broken. For weeks on end they were taking everything he had, he felt like he had no choice, no way out. When the army came to collect his crops he refused, saying it was too much, working day and night for nothing. The army warned him of his fate should he disobey, but Ian had enough! He just wanted to feed his family after an honest day's work.

The next day, Ian knew what was coming for him. He was summoned by the leader.

"Goodbye, my love." He said sincerely to his wife. "I will be back before you know it." Even though he knew his fate, being imprisoned for disobeying, but he couldn't be further from the truth.

The leader in anger lashed out. "We will make an example of this man! If any of you try to disobey my ruling your fate will be the same." Just then, he struck Ian with a deadly arrow through his heart. The arrow sped across like a lightning bolt. Ian fell to the ground. Suddenly, it felt like the world was deafened by the silence. He was left lying lifeless where he fell. No one dared to move.

That evening the villagers gathered together to bury Ian in the land. People came from far and wide, with comforting touches but absolute fear in their eyes as to what would happen next. A hero, a warrior in their eyes. Victoria looked on in utter disbelief, her granddaughter Amelia by her side, gripping onto her grandmother's hand, pain etched on their faces. What had just happened? Victoria, in a split second, had lost her soulmate, her guide. What will she do? The villagers were scared into accepting the leaders demands. Who even was this new leader? They knew they had to find out. Did he start the fire at the castle that wiped out the royal family?

Chapter 3

The Final Goodbye

His grave lay solemn and bare. Through teary bloodshot eyes, Amelia stared at the large brown cross, on it her grandfather's blue cap lay, looking just as sad and lost as she felt. At this moment Amelia thought she would never be happy again. The leader was a despicable man! Amelia screamed from the inside. He and his army did this. She came to the realisation, he was gone, gone forever. What would they do? How would they survive? She and her grandmother's lives had changed forever. Would their lives ever go back to any form of normality? Her head was full of fear. Would she be killed next? Would her Grandmother be killed? Had the army taken over the farm? The only thing other than working on the farm that Amelia was good at was mending clothes. Before she left for the graveyard, her grandmother told her that everything would be okay, but she just couldn't see how it ever would be.

She fell to her knees. The pain was so overwhelming. Amelia felt her heart beating out of her chest. Her grandfather was her whole world, her protector. She could feel a fire burning up inside her. Why did this have to happen?! Ian was her grandfather, a tall, broad man with piercing blue eyes that twinkled in the morning sun. He had shining brown hair, but as he got older grey speckles appeared. His farm meant everything to him, he used his crops to feed and provide for his family. They weren't a wealthy family, but what they lacked in money they made up for with love.

The clouds parted and the sun shone, a white feather fell from the sky. It was like it fell from heaven. Amelia took some comfort in this, a sign maybe from Grandfather Ian that everything was going to work out in the end. Walking in the warm, blinding sun, Amelia was thinking of what to do next. She missed her grandfather terribly but she had to ensure her grandmother was safe, she felt she must take over her grandfather's place at home. She had to get back to see what was happening to the land and to see if the new leader had destroyed all of the crops. Who was this new

17

leader and where did he come from? There was no one she could get guidance from as the Royal family were all killed in the fire and her grandfather wasn't here to help anymore. Was this the doing of this new leader and his army? Was the fire a terrible accident or were they responsible? Amelia could feel her heart racing. There were so many unanswered questions.

On the peak of the hill was an apple tree. Amelia picked an apple, the reddest apple she had ever seen, and sat looking afar, contemplating what to do next. It felt like she could see for miles and miles. The ash from the burning castle was still dancing in the sky in the distance. The sun was going down, she had to get home to her grandmother. One last goodbye first she thought, running down the hill as fast as her feet would take her. "I love you Papa!" she shouted as loud as she could.

Chapter 4

Unfortunate Meetings

It was a sunny afternoon, An emaciated teenage boy with short curly brown hair, and dull blue eyes who was average height and a slim woman with long black hair tied into an elegant bun with dark brown eyes were staring at their friend's grave in anger. The grey granite headstone is a rectangular shape with a slight eclipse on top. It had a small wooden cross made from pine, with the friend's name on it. There was a small bouquet of pink carnation flowers. "He should NOT have died!" they thought to themselves. "It is all that new leader's fault! He will pay for what he has done, " they thought silently.

In sheer rage and anger, the boy kicked the dirt and grass next to his friend's tombstone, sending a cloud of mud, grass, and little pebbles flying into the air. This ended up enraging Amelia who was in a black dress adjacent to him. "What was that for?!" she yelled at them, with tones of anger and disbelief. "It was an accident, sorry, " the boy apologies.

"Better hope it was!" Amelia shouted.

"It was an accident okay, just calm down, " the woman explained. The graveyard had a bitter yet tense atmosphere. 4 crows were perched on gravestones a few metres away. They seemed to be watching the 3 of them with their cold black eyes, seemingly staring into their soul. Amelia, noticing these crows, was curious to why the crows were staring at them. She was slightly panicked by these crows so she picked up a couple of stones from the cold graveyard floor and threw them at the crows, scaring them off, and they flew away, never to return. Amelia turned back to the boy and woman.

"I'm sorry for shouting it is just that my grandfather died a few days ago." Amelia began to tear up. "Our friend also passed just because he was saying how unjust it is taking over half of the farmer's crops and he was saying that the royals were a much better leader." "How did your grandfather die?" the woman asked.

"It was because he couldn't give handover more than half of his crops to the leader, as my grandfather wanted us to have food and be able to get more money. S-so he

S-sacrif-ficed him sel-lf so we didn't have to give up half-f of our crops. "Amelia was bawling at the unfairness of her grandfather's death. "They had to imprison him to make an example of him. They didn't even let him say goodbye!"

"We are very sorry for your loss, " the boy and the woman said sympathetically. The sun began to fade away, you could see the castle. If you looked hard enough you were also able to see the burnt-down wing from the graveyard along with the great church. They all had a depressed expression and mood as they grieved their loss, neither knowing what to say to one another. "So uh what is your name?" the boy asked. "Amelia Suddleton, so what are you two called?" Amelia questioned.

"My name is Werner Weidefield but you can call me Wern" the boy answered,

"and my name is Charlotte Clifton, " the woman replied.

"So, how do you think the new leader is?" Wern whispered.

"Absolutely, awful, atrocious, abysmal, appall-..." Amelia said in rage.

"Ok ok, we get the picture you absolutely hate him. So do we, just keep it down, someone might hear us, " Charlotte whispered. "I don't know why but he seems to be very mysterious. I mean he has hardly shown his face at all! Most of the villagers don't even know his name. It is like he is hiding something. And apparently everything he does is what the Royals would have wanted. I'm not buying it, " Charlotte added on. "We can't let him just kill innocent civilians!"

He also doesn't seem to care about the people of the kingdom, we have to do something!" Wern yelled.

"Be quiet Wern. As I was going to say, yes, we can't let him do this, but what can we do to stop him? There are only 3 of us, " Charlotte quietly said.

"We could try to find a living heir to the throne.

If people know there is a living heir, they might help us overthrow the leader or we could rally members of the village by telling them what the new leader has done to innocent people, " Amelia suggested.

"I can't stay here for much longer as I have to go before my grandmother gets worried about where I went. "Amelia took her black leather bag and began to walk on the well-maintained gravel path towards the Victorian-style cast iron gate which was painted as black as the graveyard lit by moonlight. "Wait, Amelia! Will we see you again?" the two asked simultaneously.

"I suppose we can come here again soon at a similar time okay?" Amelia responded. "Okay see you soon!" Wern enthusiastically said. Amelia began to walk out of the graveyard on her way back to her grandmothers house.

Chapter 5

The Fall of the Farmlands

Since the start of the new ruling many farmers started to struggle as major changes were felt on the farm. The farmlands had gone from flourishing fields to parched patches in the space of a couple of weeks. They were dry to a crisp, crops stopped growing and were destroyed and vegetation went dry, leading to the destruction of many farmlands. However, when questioned about this, the leader seemed unfazed, and reassured the public that all of his efforts and measures were for the benefit of the people and for the village. The leader's argument was that crops weren't up to their usual performance standards because of the time of year and that the village was experiencing a rather cold and harsh winter. This led to the silence of many people throughout the village who had kept their faith in the new leader, however, Amelia wasn't convinced. For her, this was all a massive trick by the new leader. Amelia was convinced that the new leader was one who only cared for himself and no-one else. She also had a different view on matters with the farmlands, as there were certain crops that could still grow at this time of year and the village has managed to still grow crops in winters a lot more brutal than this one. Amelia's grandfather would explain to her when she was younger, "It is never impossible. A crop can always succeed under the right care no matter the circumstances." Her grandfather always had this mindset and practically every time he was correct and he would succeed.

Amelia felt that the new leader didn't care about the agricultural side of the village and took all the best crops for himself, giving very little back to the farmers whether that be recognition, money, or resources. Amelia felt especially passionate about this considering that this was her late grandfather's trade of work. "Since the new rule, the farmers are the true foundation of this village, without them we would crumble beyond imagination, " Amelia would explain. She believed the farmers were the slowly crumbling concrete of the village. The concrete wasn't receiving the maintenance it needed to keep the village together.

Amelia and her new friends had all agreed previously that the new leader had no relations to the previous royal family as, if he did, it would've been in his best intentions to help the farmers to produce top-quality crops and to help their fields flourish. This obviously wasn't the case and their suspicions had been victorious over them to conclude that the new leader wasn't for the people and in fact had no relations to the previous royal family. They had all explained to each other, "The only relation that this man would have to the royals is being their worst enemy".

However, it wasn't only the farmers that had felt the effects of the new ruling. The general public was also feeling affected. People complained of tightened security around the streets when there were no such requirements and people's thoughts, views and opinions did not look to be in the best passions of the new leader. When compared to the previous royals, this new leader enraged many and there were split views on his leadership capabilities throughout the kingdom. It wasn't just his qualities that were intimidating. It was also his spine-shivering appearance. A tall man with pale skin, blue eyes, and a beard, doesn't give an impression of the easily approachable and you can feel comfortable enough to explain of all your complications and requirements to' type of person.

The farmers felt a sense of fear that their crops might not perform in the spring which is most certainly the prime time of the year for crops to grow, vegetation to succeed and new life to be born. However, without this, the farms of the village would be on a rapid downhill decline. Farmers of the village were very good at communicating with each other and the conversations would always massively involve discussions of the crop's potential for the new year. "I'm not going to be able to produce enough to feed my family never mind a whole village, " were the cries of many angered farmers. On some days they would even propose strike action and would hold up banners reading, "Let our farms thrive or you'll struggle to stay alive." This was a deterrent which was obviously aimed at that of the new leader. The farmers continued to show their rage as the new leader continued to tell them, "When the season comes around our farms will flourish and your frowns will be turned upside down so I suggest you keep working as your selfish strikes will only cause more harm to you and your fellow villagers. " The farmers were clearly enraged by this choice of speech. In all the villagers' eyes there was only one truly selfish being and that of course was the cruel, heart-of-stone leader who now, of course, had rule over this village and was sending it on a swift decline as a result of his selfish choices and actions.

All the villagers could agree that since the start of the new rule the village had gone from a wonderful wonderland to a controversial kingdom. "Its went from dreamland to hell!" cried some villagers. "It's an open jail cell, any of our luxuries or pleasures are all surrendered to the king! It truly is hell on earth!" roared others. It wasn't the life they deserved. But they had a leader who never cared about what they required, they had a leader who never catered to their views and opinions, they had a leader who was sending them on a downhill ride and was going to leave them with an uphill conflict. Would that be against him or would it be a revival of the village? They did not know yet, however, they had a plan. A plan that they were assured and certain would work, a plan that motivated them to get their village back, a plan that motivated them to bring their democratic views back, a plan that would deliver them the life that they all deserved. We have a plan, we will get our freedom, happiness, farmlands, and friends back we will get the life that we all deserve!' was their motto and motivation to get. What they wanted and rightfully deserved.

Chapter 6

The Market Place

Charlotte, Wern, and Amelia are at the marketplace in the village.

Amelia, Charlotte, and Wern all decided to head to the marketplace located near the burnt-down Lazurite Palace, that was still partially standing, despite its wretched condition. They wanted to try and acquire more information on who burnt down the palace and why they did it. The market was bustling with life, people were singing and dancing. Traders were selling all kinds of foods, clothes and fabrics at their stalls. Children were running around playing tag and laughing together.

"Even after the great loss of the royal family, the marketplace is still thriving. It's still the same, even after all these years, " Charlotte said, with a soft smile on her face.

"We should still be alert! There are all kinds of people that hang out in the marketplace, " Wern said in a blunt and serious tone.

"You're right. Let's just try to get as much information on the castle and the royal family as possible, and leave, " Amelia spoke, wanting to get the information that was needed and leave as soon as possible.

They all nodded in agreement and started to devise a plan. Which was immediately interrupted by the loud sound of horns and drums playing in the distance. An army of soldiers started marching through the village, towards the marketplace. One of the soldiers, who was wearing shiny silver armor and had a long elegant sword in hand, marched to the centre of the marketplace and blaringly announced, "Make way for the King!"

Amelia, Charlotte, and Wern were all startled by the sudden change of events. All the people in the market stopped what they were doing and turned to face the soldier. Amelia, Charlotte and Wern all had an uneasy feeling from this. The marketplace that was bustling with life not so long ago became dead silent, almost like a ghost town. Wern had a suspicion, so he grabbed Amelia and Charlotte by the wrist and ran with them to hide behind a stack of large wooden crates. Amelia,

Charlotte and Wern were all crouched down, hiding behind the large crates.

The three were silent, not making a single sound as they watched the soldier who had a solid expression on his face. The soldier seemed to be as cold as ice. He was practically a statue. Amelia whispered in a hushed tone, "What is happening?!"

"Shhh! Be quiet! Do you want them to see us!" Wern had a stern expression, he seemed focused. His dull blue eyes were fixated on the soldier. Amelia and Charlotte also cautiously observed the soldier. The soldier started to march in a full circle around the market, before coming to a halt and moving into position. After the soldier had gotten into position, another army of soldiers marched into the market single-file, before splitting up and getting into positions. Soldiers were now spread out, surrounding the entire market.

One of the soldiers announced to the public again, "Make way for the King!"

All the soldiers stamped in unison, and held

their swords up high into the air. A tall, frail old man, with a long beard and hair as black as coal slowly emerged. He had pale blue eyes that could emit fear into anyone. He was someone of a higher rank. The old man stood tall. His hands were behind his back as he slowly walked towards the centre of the marketplace. Everyone in the marketplace bowed down to this new King. The old man was now standing at the centre of the marketplace, he put his arms in the air and proudly announced to the public in a rather brittle voice, "Good evening everyone! I'm sure you all have heard about the tragic news of the fire. That has unfortunately taken the lives of our beloved Monarchy. Now you all may be wondering, who will rule our village now? Well, I'm sure most of you have already heard the news, that I'll be your new King!" All the people clapped and cheered once they heard this news, Amelia, Charlotte and Wern on the other hand, weren't really sure what to think of this. The new king seemed to already be an old and frail man. Was he really fit for this big of a responsibility?

Charlottes eyes widened in surprise as she let out a gasp. Amelia and Wern turn to look at Charlotte with a look of concern. Charlotte whispers, "I-I recognise that man he was the royal advisor Fredrickson Fitzwilliam"

"Really!? Maybe he knows what happened to the Royal Family!" Amelia gasped, she couldn't believe it.

"Amelia no! Stay down! He seems suspicious don't you think?" Wern was still focused on the soldier along with this new "King".

Amelia sighed, before nodding her head. He was right after all. This new "King" didn't really look that approachable or someone that you could talk to. The man had a cold and somewhat unsettling appearance. His facial features were quite sharp, and he was pale and almost looked dead.

The new "King" started to give orders to soldiers. The soldiers all marched off to do what they were told. During this, something caught Amelia's attention. A young man with a muscular build had soft copper-colored hair tied back into a ponytail with amber eyes. He was locked up in a cage behind the new "King". He seemed to be a prisoner. Two soldiers were guarding it. Amelia whispered, "Guys, look! That man is locked up in that cage! We should help him!"

"But how? What if they kill us!" Charlotte seemed somewhat apprehensive, of the safety of both Amelia and Wern.

"Let's just leave him in there, if he's in there it's probably because he did something horrendous. He'll probably try to backstab us if we help him, " Wern said in a snarky tone.

"Oh c'mon Wern! You don't know if he's bad? He could have been framed or put in that cage for no reason!" Amelia slightly raised her voice.

"Now now everyone calm down why don't we give him the benefit of the doubt? Let's not prejudge people, Wern, hm?" Charlotte looked at Wern to see if he'd give the lockedup person a chance. Wern was about to say something else but decided to stop himself.

"Fine! We'll give the guy a chance But if he betrays us don't come crying to me about it!" Wern said in an annoyed and slightly irritated tone.

"Yes!" Amelia was ready to rescue the man. She got into a stance, her eyes fixated on the cage and guards.

"Hmmm we need to devise some sort of plan.." Wern mumbled. Wern was now deep in thought. The three silently thought of a strategy, on how to distract the guards and free the prisoner. An idea popped into Wern's head, and he started to explain the plan to both Amelia and Charlotte. Charlotte and Amelia were going to cause some havoc near the stalls, by knocking and throwing things towards the guard's general direction, while staying anonymous. Wern was then going to snatch the keys off the guards and unlock the cage, freeing the prisoner. The four of them would then meet up behind these large wooden crates. All three of them nodded in agreement to this plan since it was the best idea they could think of.

Amelia and Charlotte both swiftly grabbed whatever they could find from the stalls and started throwing it at the guards, as the two tried to hide behind the large pots and crates. The guards stamped their feet and unsheathed their long swords and held them up high. They started marching towards the direction of where the items were coming from. Wern briskly got a hold of the keys that were dangling at one of the guard's belts. He opened the cage and quickly grabbed the prisoners wrist and ran off. Amelia and Charlotte also followed behind him once the guards were distracted. They were now all crouched down behind the large wooden crates once again. Wern spoke in an almost harsh tone, "Who are you? And why were you in that cage?" Wern was practically interrogating the guy.

Charlotte spoke, in a calm and mellow tone, "Calm down Wern. I'm sure he wouldn't cause us much trouble." Charlotte makes an attempt to de-escalate the situation.

Wern let out a sigh, as he restarted in a more

calm tone. "Why were you locked up? And what is your name?"

The prisoner was silent for a few moments but spoke up eventually. "I am Icarus Icarus Anderson and I do not know why or how I got into that cage, " he said hesitantly.

Wern narrowed his eyes at Icarus, still not trusting a word he said. Charlotte eventually spoke up. "Well, it is a pleasure to meet you Icarus. My name is Charlotte Clifton and that's Amelia." She gestured towards Amelia who proudly had her head up high as soon as her name was mentioned. "And that's Wern please excuse him he can be rather snarky at times" Wern turned his head away and pouted with his arms crossed.

Amelia looked up at the clock and mentioned, "We've been out for quite a while now let's head back to my grandmother's house. I'm sure she wouldn't mind accommodating you guys." All four of them nodded to each other. Charlotte, Wern, and Icarus all followed behind Amelia to the house while trying to avoid being spotted by the soldiers who were on patrol.

Chapter 7

The Heir

Amelia, Wern, Icarus, and Charlotte all walked
up to the reasonably humble wood and stone house

Victoria lived in. As they walked up the stone path, they heard marching soldiers in the distance. They approached the front step and knocked on the wooden door.

Victoria unhooked the metal latch and opened the front door to let them in, a welcoming smile on her face. As entered, they could smell Victoria making one of her favourite meals as they walked through the hall; chicken, carrots, and parsley. In the hallway, they could see many pots, plants, and some trinkets. The floor was old and extremely creaky as the group made their way along it. Charlotte slipped away from the group, going upstairs to bed. The stairs creaked as Charlotte climbed up them. The remaining friends walked through the open doorway and made their way into the cozy living room.

Inside the room were a couple of old couches with some basic cushions. There were also a few cushioned chairs with a nice view of the farm from the bay window. There was a picture of Ian sat on the coffee table, and they all shared a feeling

46

of safety and community as they sat down.

Victoria, with a cup of tea in her hand, a happy atmosphere, and a beaming smile, started to tell them about the fact there might be an heir to the throne. "There is some exciting news I have to tell you all." Even though Victoria was eager, her voice was still soft and quiet.

"What is it?" Amelia questioned.

"I have been told there might be an heir to the throne." Once the friends heard this, they were shocked, they couldn't believe there might be an heir to remove the new leader from power and return the village to its old state.

In disbelief, Amelia asked: "Is this true?"

"Of course it is! Can you believe it?" Victoria exclaimed.

"Do you know where the heir is?" Wern questioned.

"I think the heir will possibly be locked up in the east wing of the castle, in the wing that burnt down."

Icarus looked confused, "Won't we need a good

plan to get in though?"

"I think we should do it in the dead of night, so we are much less visible, " Amelia explained. Two doves can be seen sitting on a tree branch outside the bay window. Marching was heard in the distance once again, changing the subject to the new ruler. The doves flew off due to the loud noise, Victoria noticing this was visibly saddened by the majestic doves soaring off.

They started to rant about how bad the new leader is, and how there are more guards than ever who patrolled the streets.

"Don't you remember how good life was before the new leader? You didn't have to give a percentage of your crops to them, the taxes were not as high, and you didn't feel as imprisoned." Victoria frowned.

"This is why we need to find the heir to make things like they used to be!" Amelia said, determined.

"Indeed." Icarus replied.

"Before you go, shall I tell you about how life

was, much before the fateful day?" Victoria suggested.

"Of course, " they all say in agreement.

"Once upon a time, the kingdom was ruled by the royals and has been ruled by them for centuries they were loved by all. Every Sunday the village would gather in the great church." Victoria smiled. "The church was beautiful, it was made of granite and sandstone which was engraved with the royal name, the outside had lovely flowers and trees. The path going up to the church was made of fine stone, the front had an enchanting grand arch. Inside, the floors were made of marble with an exquisite red carpet going down the aisle to the podium there were always flowers on the podium, and behind it was a stunning stained glass window picturing the grand war in the 15th century. The walls had magnificent stained glass windows, on them the pews were made of polished oak. This is where they would thank the Gods for their blessings. During these times there was also enough food to go around; the farms were doing

49

very well every year. When Ian wasn't working on the farm he used to sit on our front porch in his ash rocking chair, smoking his pipe. He watched the doves fly over the freshly ploughed fields where he had a stunning view of the hills, every Sunday he went to the great church to thank the gods after church we used to go swimming in the bright blue waters of the nearby lake." Victoria finished. Amelia was about to open the squeaky old iron latch to the door but then she decided to go back into the living room to stay for tea.

o breat

Chapter 8

Forgotten Memories

Amelia jumps up from her seat. "What if we all go find this royal heir!" Amelia says enthusiastically. Her whole face lights up.

Wern speaks in his usual snarky tone "Hah! Do you really think the royal heir could've survived¿' He crosses his arms and rolls his eyes at Amelia, she clenches her fists in annoyance and is about to say something but, Charlotte intervenes, to try and calm down the tension. "Why don't we all get some rest? Everyone must be tired?" Everyone nods. It was exactly midnight, the moon shone brightly over the desolate farm. Amelia's grandma allowed everyone to stay at her house for the night. Amelia slept in her own bed, Icarus was sleeping on the floor with blankets and pillows by Amelias bed, Wern slept on the cushioned chair and Charlotte was sleeping on the couch. The house was quiet and peaceful. Everyone was fast asleep, except for Charlotte.

Charlotte was struggling to sleep, she was laying on the couch with her eyes wide open. Staring at the ceiling, which made creaking sounds every now and then, due to the wind. It was very quiet in the house, you could hear the faint sound of wind and the floorboards creaking. All kinds of thoughts were going through her mind. Why did the castle burn? Who would hate the royal family that much? They were loved very much by everyone in Lazurite Kingdom. Why was Icarus locked up in that cage? Will the guards catch us? Are we even safe in here? Eventually, Charlotte's eyelids grew heavy and she slowly drifted off into a deep slumber. The house was now dead silent, all that could be heard was the sounds of everyone's peaceful and slow breathing.

Charlotte's fingertips started to twitch, Charlotte was tossing and turning. She was a having a nightmare. Charlotte was in the Lazurite palace. She was working in the kitchen, sorting out the teacups and tea on the day of the fire. She was sorting out the tea for the king and queen. The teacups and teapot were gently placed onto a long elegant golden tray, which was decorated with the finest Lazurite crystals, like everything in the castle. Charlotte picked up the tray and walked out of the kitchen and into the long endless hallway. The hallways had elegant lilac wallpaper with a regal silver flower pattern. The hallways had pictures of the Royal family and of the past generations. Charlotte would always admire these portraits as she walked by, the portraits were so detailed and intricate and had a beautiful golden frame around them. Charlotte eventually made it to the King and Queen's room, but something felt off. There was an almost eerie atmosphere. Charlotte heard the Queen crying. She reluctantly opened the door and looked through a small crack. The royal advisor had a knife in his hand. The King was lying on the floor he was dead, but you could still see the fear in the King's eyes, petrified fear would forever be on his face.The Queen started pleading and crying to the royal advisor. Charlotte was frozen in fear, she was on the verge of tears and too scared to move, too scared to make a noise, too scared to do anything. She tried to scream but couldn't. The royal advisor then lifted his knife and ended the Queen's life.

Charlotte was trembling and she struggled to breathe, she dropped the tray causing the teacup and teapot to shatter across the floor. The royal advisor jerked his head to look at Charlotte. His eyes were soulless, they were empty, and his dull blue eyes pierced through Charlotte's soul. The royal advisor picked up a chair and slowly walked towards Charlotte. Charlotte didn't move a muscle, she was petrified, she didn't know what was happening. She couldn't believe what she saw. The King trusted the royal advisor the most, out of all the staff in the palace. She felt sick to her stomach, and as the royal advisor slowly walked towards her with a sombre expression, he knocked Charlotte out with the chair. The chair smashed into pieces, and Charlotte was left there laying on the floor unconscious. She couldn't move or see. Everything was a blur. She could hear the sound of fire burning, and the screams of people she could feel the heat and warmth of the fire against her skin, the fire spread around the castle rapidly, it was so bright and beautiful Charlotte had many emotions. Fear, grief, and confusion she couldn't believe that her life was going to end at such a young age Charlotte felt sad when she thought about all the things she hasn't done in her life yet, all the places she hasn't seen

The scorching and blistering fire around her was unforgiving. It was violently burning and destroying everything in its path. The castle crumbled, and screams still echoed through the halls. People were jumping through windows, breaking down doors everyone was desperate to escape, but Charlotte was left there left to die the palace was empty, no one was in the palace with Charlotte except for one Wern came running down the hallway. "Charlotte! Charlotte! Where are you?!" He screamed in desperation. He was scrambling around trying to find Charlotte. Charlotte slowly opened her eyes, everything was a blur. She tried to speak, she tried to scream Wern I'm here! I'm here!' But nothing came out. Wern eventually saw Charlotte laying on the floor unresponsive, he rushed to Charlotte and threw her over his shoulder. Wern carried Charlotte to safety. Charlotte couldn't remember what happened after that

Charlotte then woke up in a cold sweat, she was breathing heavily, and tears filled her eyes. Charlotte started to break down in tears, She remembered everything that happened in the fire it was a coverup the royal advisor assassinated the royal family but used that fire to hide it. "Why! Why! Why didn't I do something?! I just watched them get murdered right in front of me!" Charlotte screeched. Charlotte screamed at the top of her lungs as she bawled her eyes out. She gets off the couch and storms out of the house, leaving the door wide open. Everyone jerks awake and looks at the open door, everyone was concerned about Charlotte.

"Is Charlotte okay!" Amelia exclaims, looking worried.

"C'mon! Let's go and check on her to see if she's alright." Wern says in a calm yet slightly concerned tone. Wern and Amelia get up and

rush out the door to check on Charlotte. Icarus
followed sombrely behind.

Chapter 9

Moonlight Walks

Icarus is the last one of them out of the small hut, as he shuts the door he catches a glimpse of

Victoria, her demeanour unlike this shambles of a home is strong. Her shoulders set, head held high, she might be small but she is mighty, like her granddaughter. Her eyes meet his, the same bright hazel as Amelia's, bright as the sun and twice as proud. She smiles at him the way a mother would smile at their child. The door shuts clicking behind him leaving Victoria and her warmth inside. Icarus leaves all his guilt and his sorrow inside and marches to the only people who have ever truly accepted him into a death trap.

"Come on Icarus, this isn't an evening stroll. This is the start of a revolution for the ages! And you wont believe what charlotte just told us " he bet he would " The fire was staged by Ferdrickson to cover up the fact that he killed the Royal family"

Icarus plastered on his best cocky grin, the same one he had been wearing for the last couple of days, and said " Cant say I am suprised he was no good from the start.And come on A revolution? Without me, you wont make it past the gate."

"The gate? Now who said anything about the gate? We will go through the window, rendering you useless, Icarus!" Wern told him as he walked backwards, staring up at the moon with a wishful look in his eyes. Icarus was about to crush that hope. He was going to crush Wern's hopeful nature, Demolish Charlotte's kindness and he was going to devastate Amelia's pride. So as he closed his eyes and allowed the night air to in-compass his sense the smell of the fisherman's fresh catch blowing from the east, the sea smelt the same as it had when he was a child of brine and freedom, the feeling of the air ruffling his hair, the sight of his friends and the beautiful village that surrounded them full of buildings built by hand each one, build ground up with the sweat, blood, and tears of the people. As they passed Ms Appletons he felt his mouth water at the mere thought of her delicious apple pies he had tried on his first day with this odd group of people. They also walked by a small flower garden filled to the brim with flowers. Flowers of all colours from the brightest red to the inkiest blue, the serene garden had been erected in honor of Amelia's grandfather, he had helped plant those flowers, that had held Amelia as she cried out all of the loss here. He was sick, oh well he had accepted that long ago. The moonlight reflected off of all these beautiful sights making this small village feel ethereal.

Beautiful sights that would soon reek of nothing but despair and content, content towards him. He reflected all of this in the deepest parts of his mind. Smiling he did not utter a word the rest of the journey allowing these last moments of peace to feel like a whole world but he couldn't stay forever. So as they approached the castle it was gone, that peaceful world shattered by sorrow-filled reality. He smiled at his lost strode with the mission he was born to complete, bidding goodbye to the beautiful, ethereal essence of mundane life.

The East wing which was once adorned with gold ringlets around tall slender windows and flagged by alluring guardian angel statues. Was now nothing short of something out of a nightmare. The once majestically built building was reduced to his foundation of wooden pillars coated with mere fractions of charred bricks. The Guardian angel's face melted giving away the illusion that they were screaming, Icarus found this almost amusing like they had seen some great horror and were forever stuck in shock, well at least the royal family will have company. Wern went to step out of the shadows they were protected by and towards the nightmare building, but before he could Icarus shot his arm out stopping him.

"Guards, " he whispered to the group of guards currently coming around the behind of the broken building. Six in total clad in the new uniforms courtesy of New King Fredrickson. They, much like the east wing, had changed from a safe presence to one to be feared, from the black metal shoulder pad-like knives to their boulder-shaped helmets with a single black feather sticking out from the top a horrible attempt to class these brutish Neanderthals, the guards.

"Theyre like an overzealous peacock" piped up

Charlotte.

"What's a peacock¿' questioned Wern and Amelia in twin confusion.

"Something I read about in one of the visiting Nobel lady's books. They're birds, Oh, they are stunning. With big feathers with all kinds of colors throughout them." Charlotte finishes with a dreamy look on her face.

Amelia and Wern "ooh" and "ahh" at this explanation, and Icarus is struck with the shocking reminder that once again these people with such big ideas and dreams for this world are some of the poorest educated in the country.

Snapping out of his thoughts Icarus calls the group back to their objective "We will need to move fast, before the next group of guards comes around we have approximately 35 seconds. Once this group makes it around the next bend we have to wait about 25 seconds longer."

"How do you know all this?" Charlotte asked.

All eyes turned to him standing out in the shadows, For a second just a second Icarus felt like a being of prey surrounded by predators, like a wolf in sheep's clothing being closed in by the rest of the herd. He took a deep breath and allowed the feeling to subside before answering, "I came by last night and timed it, " he managed to get out all the words in an even tone, and he waited for their reply.

"Oh good thinking, Icarus¡' Charlotte said in a cherry tone before Amelia jumped into her plan for what to do once they were inside. He was close, Icarus was so close, only a few more lies, a few more tales to spin and it would be over. For them at least. He was so close so when he saw the last sliver of black feathers disappear around the bend. He felt relief.

Relief? He wanted to scream; he was about to betray people who were trusting their lives with him, and he felt relief.

Before he could question himself further: "Look, the guards are gone, quick!" Amelia said, grabbing Icarus by his arm and leading him forward with no fear. Just a clear objective in mind. As they slipped off and into the darkness and towards the house of the screaming angels, he was once again in awe of this girl; so young, so strong. It really was a shame she had to die. Scaling the castle walls was easier than Icarus had thought. Sure, he knew where the guards would be, what bricks to step on and what ones not to step on, but it was the rest of the group that had surprised him. They didn't know which bricks to step on and what ones not to, what supports were stronger than others.

No, they climbed on pure instinct to survive, to conquer, to avenge, to win. It was indeed an interesting feat to watch: like seeing lions battling out for the top of the pride. Once they had reached the top, Wern chipped in with one of and as always helpful comments: "Well, who is surprised, the murder house is just as creepy on the inside as the outside."

With this Charlotte handed over her favourite hairpin to Amelia, tucking out of hair with visibly frustration while glaring at Wern. "What was that about?" Icarus asked.

"Hey Charlotte, I bet that scaredy-cat over there, would make up some bad joke to hide the fact that he was scared within the first ten seconds of getting in, " Amelia says.

"3 more seconds and we would have been in the clear, you dolt." Charlotte says, punching Wern's arm playfully. Icarus can't suppress the laugh that arises.

Even though it was a bad attempt to hide his fear, Icarus thought he wasn't wrong, the inside of the east wing mirrored the outside with its broken windows, creaking and damp floorboards the room only lit by the moonlight outing in throughout the glass shards. To think this was once a vibrant home. The Royals may have been a ruling monarchy but they were still a family, all of this felt like a preview of what it would be like with The new king as a plague across the land sucking it dry of life and happiness.

"Right, now that I have been thoroughly embarrassed may we please get on with finding our little lost sovereignty." Wern said blushing deeply, but at the mention of our little lost sovereignty' and his small epiphany about what he was a part of, Icarus' happiness was broken, replaced with the tight feeling that tightened around his heart.

"Right, we should get going, " Icarus said soberly. With that they journeyed deeper into the once vibrant home. four people. However, little did they know only one of them would be leaving the fallen East wing of Lazurite Castle.

Chapter 10

Search of the Charred Building

Everyone clambered in one after another, Amelia going first. She found herself in what she assumed was a small living room. It was a vast space, decorated with floral patterns and rich-looking furniture. It was a shame that it looked so damaged; it must have been gorgeous before. When the whole group was inside, they walked to the door opposite them. It led to a beautiful hallway, which complimented the living room perfectly. Although slightly mangled, the floral pattern continued but now with red accents. It led their eyes to one door, which Amelia felt herself enchanted by. She led the group to it and found a dining area. "Wow..." she whispered, looking around the elegant room, focusing on the long wooden table in the middle. It was adorned with a charming red cloth which matched the curtains. There were intricate and careful details carved out on each piece of furniture which, no doubt, took lots of time and effort to make. She had never seen anything this refined or affluent in her life. She was stunned.

"We should move, " Wern said hurriedly, interrupting her train of thought. He looked around the room as though he didn't get her amazement. "We haven't got all day."

They nodded in unanimous agreement. Wern led them out into one of many long hallways. As they treaded through them, Amelia noted the walls had many paintings of people, young and old, but some sections were empty. "They must be taking these down, " she thought sombrely. They continued at a steady pace, and every so often Charlotte or Wern would suggest a room, but they hadn't found anything so far. This continued until they heard heavy footsteps approaching behind them. Hearts dropped as they shared a look of sheer horror and anxiety. Icarus reassured them it was their imagination but still, the friends silently began to run, finding themselves turning and rushing through long hallways before finally piling into a room around a corner.

It was unclear what the point of the room they had rushed into was, or why it existed. It was the size of a bedroom yet only housed a single armchair. The chair was bright green, contrasting heavily with the red walls. It felt out of place although the whole room did and the red pillow that rested on it was a weak attempt to make it fit in. Amelia breathed heavily in and out, exhausted and on edge. She glanced at her companions, who, more or less, were all in the same state as her. Charlotte was on her toes, glancing around for any sign of a guard, letting herself calm down when she found nothing. Wern was gasping labored breaths and leaning on a wall, uncaring if he saw a guard at that moment. Icarus sat down on the chair exhausted and sighed loudly. The dejected looks of them only frustrated Amelia more. Tension was thick, and the group were at their breaking point.

"Where is the heir?!" she finally fumed, ignoring the 'shush from someone behind her. She glowered harshly at the floor. Wern, still up and close with the buildings infrastructure, caught his breath.

"Clearly, not in here, " he sneered, much to

Charlotte's chagrin.

"Now is not the time for a petty argument, " Charlotte said reticently, tightening her bun. "We should rest for a moment. Breaks are important, and we will get less careful if we are exhausted." Icarus nodded, but the suggestion fell on deaf ears as Wern and Amelia continued to scowl at each other. Icarus frowned at them but didn't intervene.

"We keep going in circles! If we keep doing this, we'll never find the heir!" Amelia concluded bluntly.

Wern wavered, and Icarus looked away. "Stop being so pessimistic! It's too early to decide that, " he claimed angrily.

"I'm not being a pessimist!" She stomped, which made everyone jump at her volume. She quietened her voice and added, "I am being a realist."

"Stop this." Charlotte shut them down. "It's a miracle your petty argument hasn't gotten us caught." She spoke sternly, but not angrily.

That got their attention, and both Wern and Amelia surrendered.

"We should continue, " Icarus segued, his eyes narrowing in on the door.Charlotte agreed, forcefully making Wern and Amelia agree too.

Charlotte fronted the group, leading them through the castle, weaving through each hallway strategically, searching every nook and cranny. Anger continued to build inside Amelia as every place they checked was rendered useless. No one could find anything even referencing an heir. A crestfallen Charlotte brought an infuriated Amelia, a melancholic Wern, and a distracted Icarus back to the room they entered from.

Chapter 11

Strawberry Jam and Secrets

"What's going on? I don't understand!¿' Amelia
screeched and paced around the small room everyone found themselves in once again.It's almost
over, just a little longer Icarus thought. He had
notified the guards in the living room. They have
been following them since then. Icarus should
have given the order to intercept them there but
he couldn't bring himself to do it. Making sure
he was last out of ever room, signalling one more
room, only one more room. There were no more
rooms. It was almost over, the guards would be
here any minute and then it really would be over.

"Calm down Amelia, there must be an explanation! Maybe we missed a room, " Charlotte
cooed, trying to calm everyone down.

"We didn't, " Icarus spoke up. "We didn't
miss a room, there are no secret passageways.
There is nothing, no more clues, nothing." Icarus's
words mimicked his thoughts, but he wasn't talking about the heir. There was nothing left. The
game was over.

"No! I don't believe it! Maybe the heir is

inside the main part of the castle, we should check! Please this can't be it!" Wern pleaded.

No, Icarus thought. You can't go he can't let them leave.

"No, it's far too dangerous. The main castle will be crawling with guards and no offense, Wern I don't think they will be widely impressed by your ability to curl your tongue. Let's face it; we have lost. I mean, what were thinking? We are a group of kids! A stable boy, " Amelia muttered, looking to Wern. "A maid, " she whispered looking at Charlotte, who, to her credit, kept her head high. "An outlaw, " her voice barely audible as she looked at Icarus, her hazel eyes meeting his amber ones, god, Icarus thought, she looks so tired. "And a farmer." She said, placing her hand over her heart. Silence enveloped the room, despair was heavy just like Icarus had known it would be. It was time, Icarus was standing the furthest from the door. Everyone else had their backs to it. Amelia was by the window, and Charlotte and Wern were facing Icarus. No one saw the door open, No one saw Captain James Gordon flagged by Lieutenant Karen and Jack enter the room. Only Amelia saw Icarus raise his hand above his head and oh god, a hand has never felt so heavy. As he turned his head he caught himself in the window reflection, he looked like his father. At that single glance, that fraction of a moment, suddenly he is eight years old again, watching his father kill his mother.

Icarus looks down at his hands, all covered in red, dripping onto the floor. Oh no. Fathers going to be mad. "Oh sweetie, what have you done? You've gotten strawberry jam all over the floor" Alice, Icarus' mother cooed, picking him up and placing him on the kitchen counter and began to hum lowly trying to pacify him. "What is wrong sweetie? Why are you crying? "Alice asked.

"I thought you were father, I thought he would be mad, he is always so mad, " Icarus confessed.

"Oh honey, your father is just stressed, It's difficult being one of the top advisors to our gracious king Alice said, smiling softly but don't worry,

78

he loves you so much, he just"

A voice cut through their peace. "ALICE" Fredrickson yowled.

"Go quickly!" Alice spoke in a rush as she picked up her son, before lowering him to the floor near the door. "Go outside." she muttered, pointing to the door that led to the garden. "I will come join you soon, I will just have a word with your father."

Icarus knew it was wrong, but as he reached the door, he turned and buckled down until all that was visible was the top of his head, and peeked through the gap in the door.

"HOW COULD YOU!? I TRUSTED YOU ALICE, I TRUSTED YOU!" Fredrickson yelled. He was furious. You could feel the anger leaking out of him, infecting the once joyful environment.

"What are talking about¿' Alice questioned desperately.

"I know." Fredrickson replied, glaring at her.

"Know what¿' Alice contested.

"I know¡' Fredrickson shouted, overpronouncing each syllable of the short words. Alice paled but all Icarus saw was his father raising his hand before he was dragged away by one of the servants. The servant didn't speak even when he pleaded for answers, none were ever given. His father didn't look him in the eyes after that, he didn't even speak to him.

"Father's hands are covered in strawberry jam" Icarus whispered to himself when he saw his father, later that evening. His mother was never mentioned again, no matter how much he begged he was ignored at every attempt until the memory of his mother faded into that place dreams go when they are long forgotten.

"Icarus what are you doing?¡' Amelia said pulling him from the memory. Icarus brought his hand down and with his hand, he slipped the mask of the horrible king's son. Prince of nothing. Enemy to all. Guards entered in a flurry of struggle and pain. Screams came from the rebels, of confusion and pain. Keeping his eyes ahead he ignored Wern's screams as he was tackled to the ground.

80

He Ignored Charlotte's cries as the guard pushed her against the wall. But what he couldn't ignore was Amelia's silence she didn't speak, as she didn't struggle. She allowed the guards to capture her, but through all this her eyes never left his. Bright and burning with pride no longer, only hatred. Hatred directed towards him, it shouldn't hurt as much as it does Icarus thought.

"You're him, aren't you?" Amelia spoke, even with her comrades and herself on her knees, her voice was as cold as ice, unwavering. "Youre his son, aren't you, ? Prince Icarus Fitzwillam." The title was wielded as a sword with intent to hurt. Icarus sidestepped her question and directed all his willpower into not comforting Charlotte, who had tears streaming down her face.

"For your crimes against the Crown, I: Prince Icarus Fitzwilliam, first prince of Lazurite, " Icarus proclaimed his voice cold as steel, even if he was breaking on the inside. "I hereby sentence you to death by ... Fire."

Silence, and then screams. "how could you

81

do this!?", "What's wrong with you!¿', and "You monster!" were the insults thrown.

"What about the heir?! You wouldn't hurt a child¡' Amelia screamed at him.

"There is no heir, there never was. I just had to get you to the castle. To make an example of you, so no one else will dare rise against the crown again." Icarus said all the words he had been fed, words his father has whispered in his ear

What if what if What ifs had plagued him? "You have to understand, I had to"

Before Icarus could finish Amelia swirled on her knees, knocking Lieutenant Jacks's hands off her shoulder before grabbing the hairpin she had won off Charlotte and thrusting it into his eye. Lieutenant Jack screamed and, before anyone could stop her, Amelia threw the window open and jumped.

She landed on a stack of hay below and ran. Disappearing into the shadows. Icarus ran to the window just in time to see her take off. The moon-light reflected off her skin as she ran towards the coming dawn. Icarus couldn't control the small smile that took over his face as he watched her go, like a princess running from the evil monster.

"She won't return, " he said to the room, returning to his icy cold demeanor, but a voice inside whispered yes she will and you want her too.

Chapter 12

Chain of Disastrous Events

After Wern and Charlotte got arrested after being betrayed by Icarus, Amelia sprinted back from the stone castle with tears rolling down her cheeks. She struggled to see in the pitch black, she was unable to see even her two feet in front of her. In the distance she could hear the royal guards sweeping the village, checking every house and alleyway as they went forward, the guard's voices were getting closer and closer. Amelia was horrified but then she felt a rush of adrenaline pulsating through her veins as she bolted back to her grandmother's home. Running through the cobblestone alleyways and narrowly avoiding food waste and barrels of water she almost slipped on a wet cleaning product which caused her to stammer. Amelia ran through the main road where a crow was perched on an apple cart staring once again, Amelia didn't notice it as she was running. She then passed the flower gardens she saw on the way in, she stopped for a second to catch her breath, she was breathing heavily; Amelia was sweating like a pig. However, she could hear a group of guards armed with blades right beside her Amelia ducked behind a bramble bush. She was mortified; she prayed that the guards wouldn't find her.

"I see someone... AFTER THEM!" A soldier dressed in iron armor screamed out. Amelia thought it was over and that she was going to be caught. To her surprise, However they ran past once the noise went down to a whisper. She looked around to check if any guards were in the vicinity and then began running again. She finally made it out of the village and reached a rickety wooden fence. She began to climb over, however, the wood was rotten and it broke under her weight, causing her to graze her knee on a rough stone.

After this she began to run across the mucky fields. It was difficult to keep her balance and not fall over into the wet soil. She looked behind her for one moment but suddenly, Amelia's foot fell into a hole, catching her foot, and making her crash through the field and fall over, injuring her ankle. She clutched it for a moment but heard a sound awfully similiar to a person. Terrified of what could be behind her, she pulled herself back up. She felt her legs aching as she ran but she pushed through the pain and kept going. Amelia could see the outline of her grandmother's home. It felt like she was running for an eternity. She was sprinting up the bumpy stone path to her grandmother's door and was too tired to stop herself.

Amelia smashed through the front door due to sheer exhaustion. After a few seconds she began to call for her grandmother. "Gran are you there!?" Amelia got no reply. She slowly got back to her feet and walked through the old house. She heard the floorboards creak with every step as she called out again, "Graaan, you there!?" Still nothing, the shelves on the hallway walls were empty, the floor was a mess; it was like a crime scene. Amelia panicked at the sight of this. She cautiously walked into the living room, leaving her muddy footprints behind her. She had noticed that all the drawers had been ransacked. Amelia walked over to the dark oak coffee table (it had a stain from where Victoria used to put her tea) and found that the picture of Ian on his wedding day had been smashed. She picked it up to inspect it. Amelia put it back on the coffee table but she didn't see her grandmother anywhere and was very worried as she felt her grandmother might be in grave danger. She slowly creeped into the kitchen. The floor was covered in dirt, rubbish, and glass along with jars of food, smashed plates, cups, and bowls. Silver cutlery was also scattered across the place, the wooden cabinets had been emptied, and as she turned the corner

Her face turned to horror as she saw small puddles of blood on the mucky stone floor. When she looked up, she couldn't move, her grandmother lay motionless on the floor propped up against the corner of the counter. An arrow had been shot straight through her heart. Victoria's clothes were a wash of red, with blood dripping onto the floor. Amelia saw a knife in her grandmother's hand. "At least she put up a fight, " she thought to herself.

Amelia was in tears as she looked at her gran. "How could they ever do this to her?" she wailed, through watery eyes. It was like a river of tears flowing onto the floor to add insult to injury. Amelia noticed that they had taken her grandmother's wedding ring and her prized necklace. She struggled to process what just happened. It seemed like all hope was lost for Amelia. She was in The depths of despair, her grandmother was gone, and her friends had been captured. Everything precious in her life was gone. She couldn't take looking at her dead gran any longer and ran out of the looted house.

Chapter 13

Breaking Point

Amelia was at her breaking point. She had sprinted away from her Grandmothers house in a flood of tears. She ran to the field that lay behind her house and released all of the emotions that had bottled up inside of her. From the shock at the castle inferno to the outrage and despair that she experienced when her grandfather and grandmother passed away, and the betrayal from Icarus. It was all let go as she screamed, as she wailed in the middle of this field all by herself. She let all the recent events and sores out in one gigantic tsunami of pain and suffering. She let out all the moments that had happened so suddenly, all the experiences that had taken a major toll on her life.

At this very moment, her mind was presenting to her a sudden re-watch of all her lowest points in life. And practically all of them were since the start of this new and very cruel leadership. Amelia cried to herself when her grandfather died and she would always say, "Life's at its lowest point for me! Surely it cannot get any worse than this!" But it would. She also lost her grandmother, she had also been betrayed by someone who she had so much trust in. Icarus. All her deepest sorrows would be caused by one person and one person only. And that person would be Fredrickson. He was the one to be held accountable for this.

It was at this moment Amelia that she knew she had to keep going, She felt a fiery flame build up inside of her, a flame of complete outrage and anger, a flame that told her she must keep going. She felt very little despair now, she had released and rebuilt that despair into rage. Her beloved grandmother and grandfather were both victims of a new cruel leadership, and since this new leadership, the village had become a cold, rocky, and burdensome location to live.

She had flashbacks of happy times in the village when the place was under a finer rule. She knew this was the life she wanted back, Amelia stood up tall up from the swampy, mucky field where she had let it all out. She still felt some sense of sorrow, but mostly rage remained. She visualised the past; the happy days, that was her motivation. That was the life she needed back.

There she stood in this mucky field feeling aggrieved, enraged, and with a bonfire burning inside of her. Here, she would announce what she had been wanting to say since the downhill decline of the village, and roaring across the field this could be heard. "For my grandparents, for the fallen farmers and their fields for my people for my friends, for my village and my hometown! I will not back down until I win!".

Amelia felt charged at this moment, she felt ready, and she felt fired. From this field you were able to look on and over at the neighbouring villages, which were usually sleepy and pretty peaceful, but not this time. Amelia gazed over to see a band of beings similar to her. With the same emotions, with the same broken hearts as her. But it was not just from her hometown that people felt this sense of rage. People from neighbouring villages had joined together, and even from a distance, you could see that they had enough.

A flame of fury hurdled towards their village,

a flame that was also affected by the selfish acts of Fredrickson. Their crops had also been destroyed and they had also lost loved ones to the cruel actions of the new leader. It was at this moment Amelia realised that these people shared her emotions. They had a bond of rage, despair, and boredom all shared between them. As the band came closer, Amelia could hear chants against the new leader. It was clear that they too had enough and that the new leaders' time was up. As they marched closer to the castle, Amelia wiped away her final tears, she pulled a long piece of thick green mucky grass out of the ground and hoisted it high above her head. She let out a roar of "Vengeance!" and she sprinted down the mucky hill connecting the fields to the bumpy road ahead.

A she raced towards the marching rebellious army, she felt a sense of passion; she was joining an army to fight for what was right. She battled the powerful glares attempting to hold her back from joining a rebellion. But nothing was going to stop Amelia, not even a pot of gold.

Amelia battled through the gates as she prepared to go into battle: the battle to retake what was theirs, the battle to avenge their fallen loved ones, the battle for their fields, farmlands, and farmers, the battle for their homeland, the battle for their freedom. As Amelia joined the brave marching band she joined the chants of "Evil dies today!" which were filled with anger and fury directed towards Fredrickson, a leader who had destroyed the lives of many. The march continued towards the castle and it had only one objective, an objective that they were all determined to complete.

Chapter 14

The Angry Mob

The atmosphere was intense. A couple of village people immediately spotted her long, brown hair and cried out "She's here¡' Immediately, Amelia was pushed to the front, as villager after villager wanted her to coordinate the mob through the awkward and confusing passages inside the castle.

Realising this, Amelia yelled out from her front-ward position an incomprehensible message. Despite this, the villagers all knew it was Amelia leading, and trusted her after her tragic story had broken loose, so they blindly started to follow. The mob started frantically running up to the castle, carrying whatever makeshift weapons, from framing tools to baking utensils, they could use to oust Fredrickson. Amelia was marching the fastest, as she was staying ahead of the crowd to coordinate exactly where to lead them.

Amelia stopped before the guards who stood tall blocking the main gate. She knew it would be impossible to get through herself, because the guards were equipped with a long, pointed sword, and could easily win in a duel. Knowing this, Amelia yelled out to the even angrier crowd, "There's guards! Charge¡'. Her instructions ignited a sudden storm that had enough power to forcefully overwhelm the guards. Amelia had slipped and other furious villagers had ran ahead, but they were filled with rage and too distracted by their objective to take notice.

At this point, they had all successfully entered the castle grounds, and were on the hunt for Fredrickson. The mob steered around a bend and started chaotically running towards any door. The pack had started to break apart when Amelia, recalling her disastrous experience, steered the entire crowd to one door. She started to recall that experience again, and it ignited more hatred and anger in her mind. Amelia was determined. Determined to get revenge. Determined to kill Fredrickson. Determined to end his rule.

It was at this moment that Fredrickson realised his castle was flooded by an angry mob, who wanted him dead. After initially laughing it off, Fredrickson's chief guard alerted him they had reached the entrance to one of the areas of the castle. "They'll get lost, Im sure of it. They have no maps. All it would take would be one guard leading them the wrong way, " Fredrick stated to the guard, confident in the angry crowd's weakness. Fredrickson added, "Tell the guards to do it. Block the entrance and lead them away."

Unaware of the guard's tactics, the inferno that was the villager's temper was raging on. The fiery snake that was the mob kept sneaking around every corner, as Amelia kept shouting directions from behind. The more she thought of the unjust death of her grandparents, the strength of Fredrickson's rule over the kingdom, the betrayal by Icarus, and all the lies, the more furious she got. Meanwhile, the loud and roaring sounds of the villagers kept getting louder in Fredrickson's room. The sound went from a faint cry to a modest roar. It prompted Fredrickson, and his chief guard, to leave and take a hidden back path to another, much safer, area.

Amelia kept leading the crowd down more staircases, through more doors, and past more corri-

100

dors, when she heard the faintest sound from behind a door. It was subtle and was barely audible
over the ferocious yells of the crowd. Her mind
wandered a bit, thinking through what it could
have been, and thinking if Fredrickson would be
behind it when she heard another, more audible
and more recognisable sound. It was Charlotte.
Amelia immediately yelled into the crowd "Push
that door down!". The villagers, who were un-
sure what she was doing, blindly and forcefully
started pushing the door down. Charlotte and
Wern, who had been traumatised by the usual
sounds of guards and Fredrickson himself, were incredibly terrified as to what was about to happen.
"Wwhat's tthat¿' Charlotte quivered to Wern.

"Are we dead¿' he responded stressfully, almost like the notation would be an upgrade from
their current situation. Before any of them could
think, the door burst open, and the sudden loud-
ness thoroughly startled Charlotte and Wern. Amelia
immediately came in.

"Come with us, we're going to kill Fredrick,

" Amelia said persuasively, while she freed them and convinced them to join her.

Charlotte and Wern were completely shaken by their time in absolute isolation And darkness. At first, they were shivering with fear and were struggling to think properly. Amelia re-ignited the anger that had started in them, that hatred of Fredrickson's awful rule over the kingdom, and they re-joined the crowd with all their force and all their anger.

Amelia, Charlotte, and Wern knew the mob was close to Fredrickson's room. They couldn't hear anything but they assumed it was drowned by the anger of the villagers behind them. This was it, but as Amelia yelled out to the crowd "Charge¡', and while all the villagers came pouring in, Fredrickson was nowhere to be found. Immediately their disastrous experience came crashing into their heads. "This can't be possible, " Amelia thought, thoroughly inspecting the room for any hints of Fredrickson's location. Charlotte and Wern were losing trust in Amelia.

"Not again¡' cried Wern to Amelia.

"I don't see Icarus, so we're safe, " said Amelia, reassuringly the smallest bit sorrow evidence in her voice.

However, they knew he would be nearby. He couldn't have gone far, the villagers would have caught and killed him if he tried to escape. Amelia shouted to the crowd, "Back out, he's not here!"

As soon as Amelia said this, Charlotte ran straight for her. "I heard something! He...he's down there¡'. Amelia and Wern believed her.

"This way!" Amelia yelled out once again, "He's down here!". This stirred up the villagers even more. The pushing force by the mob suddenly increased after they heard Amelia. The crowd stormed down a corridor and started to fiercely push the door over.

Chapter 15

Revolt Against Fredrickson

The door was strong and difficult to break open. The chief guard was holding the door back, forcefully keeping the mob out of the room, but his strength couldn't hold the door shut for long. The pressure was too intense. The anger was too strong. The door creaked further, and further, until it finally, and suddenly, blew open. The door fell to the ground, crushing the guard under all the weight. They had reached Fredrickson.

For a brief moment, Amelia, Charlotte, and Wern were stunned. Fredrickson was tall, taller than they seem to remember. He stood in front of them, as stern as ever. They could hardly believe they were standing, eye-to-eye, directly in front of the man who had ignited the flame of all their anger. This was it. A chance to get revenge. A chance to bring justice back. A chance to kill Fredrickson.

While Amelia, Wern, and all the other villagers were ready to stab him, Charlotte, for a moment, questioned herself. She had known Fredrickson for a while, and almost felt bad for doing this to someone she knew so deeply, but that fear turned to anger fast as she recalled everything that had happened, from the lies about the heir to her being arrested. It all was too much, too much anger, too much injustice, too much for her to not get revenge.

Fredrickson tried to open his mouth. He knew he had little chance of survival, let alone escape, but he tried regardless. He attempted to exclaim, in his authoritative voice, "And who may you be after¿' but it was too late. The crowds had begun to push in. The storm of anger had arrived. Fredrickson just stood, looking intimidating and powerful, at the sea of rage that he had indirectly created, of villagers wanting him dead.

"Charge¡' yelled Amelia, her friends adding "Kill him!" The crowd, some equipped with weapons, others just their bare hands, began to push and charge forward, in the direction of Fredrickson. Although, Amelia heard a voice, a voice that she could not forget. A voice that she knew, not for the right reasons. A voice that filled her with more rage, betrayal, with distrust. A voice that she was in denial she could even hear. A voice that couldn't make sense. It was Icarus.

He appeared, seemingly out of nowhere, and stormed forwards in front of everyone. He was carrying a hidden sword, a sword that Amelia recognised as one of the guard's swords. He ran frantically towards Fredrickson, who was confused and enraged at his own son. Everyone, including Amelia, froze and moved aside to let Icarus charge through the crowd. He was charging at his dad, his dad whom he had loved, who he had been raised by, and who he had now hated. It all came to him, but the anger prevailed. He revealed his sword, to the horror of his dad who had not noticed, pointed it straight ahead, and spat, "I can't forgive you, father, " as he stabbed Fredrickson in the chest. The strength and speed of both Icarus and the crowd shoved Fredrickson out a window, the glass shattering to pieces, and Fredrickson stumbling out.

Everyone froze. Fredrickson was finally dead.

Ousted. Gone. The villagers nearer the back were still mad; mad over nothing, over old information, but they also froze, too, when Icarus announced to the crowd, "He's dead!", A wave of triumph started to spread, the change the villagers had demanded since news of Amelia's story spread, the revenge Amelia, Charlotte and Wern had wanted since Fredrickson had taken power, but Icarus' actions perplexed Amelia. Was he really Fredrickson's son? Was he really a fake ally? Did he really want to kill his dad so badly?

This all got more baffling because of Icarus' sudden appearance. He had came out of seemingly thin air, as Amelia never recalled seeing him in the crowd. "Why then, must he have been so desperate to kill his dad¿' questioned Amelia to herself. Icarus had started to retreat out of the castle when he heard Amelia shout his name. "Where did you come from?" she asked, loudly shouting over a small group of villagers.

Icarus replied "I'll explain later, " and swiftly started to backtrack along the endless corridors and rooms of the castle.

With a lingering sense of relief and victory, everyone retreated. The atmosphere was alive and filled with success. The way out, however, was not completely clear. Whereas before everyone blindly trusted Amelia, there was less coordination as the villagers feelings of joy overpowered any sense of organisation or reflection. Amelia, and to a lesser extent Charlotte and Wern, were celebrated. Villagers were constantly moving out of the way to let them through, despite the friends being too joyful to care. Icarus, however, had ran out as fast as he could manage. He wanted to leave immediately, despite his victorious emotions.

Once every villager had successfully navigated the maze-like castle, Amelia found Icarus sitting beside the castle, with almost no emotion except for a slight smile on his face. Amelia immediately sat down next to him. "So, where did you come from¿' she asked.

Icarus replied, in a calm and almost sad tone, "I had to do this." Amelia turned and stared as

110

if she was questioning him. Icarus added, "My father was never a good person. I've just never been
able to accept it, " he went on, as Amelia could
do nothing but stare at his shocking story. Just as
he was finishing up his story, a group of villagers
came towards them, fury presently in their eyes,
as they grabbed Icarus and spewed horrible things
about as they dragged him away. Icarus doesn't
put up a fight and Amelia doesn't stop them.

Chapter 16

Mirror or Picture?

"I can't forgive you, father." The words didn't even begin to describe the words he wanted to, should have screamed at his father. Icarus' hands were covered in strawberry jam and this time it wouldnt go away, no matter how many times he tried to wipe it. He had been trapped down here for 2 months, 3 weeks and 5 days. The cells were cramped, to put it simply. With one damp mattress in the corner, four brick walls and one small candle alight in the corner opposite to his bed', and no candle holder, you know, in case he tried to go on a murderous rampage, or, as he called it, pulling a dad'. It will be torturous in the cold months, you won't be here in the cold months, Icarus reminded himself. He had heard whispers from the Guards about the new Democracy, as they called it, ruling above. With Amelia at its head, they had assembled a table' of sorts that would be represented by one or two people from each village. All decisions would be made with complete fairness and justice towards the villages. That was all the information Icarus was able to

114

get the guards to give up. The guards also loved to sprinkle in little fun comments about their personal lives, such as the guard who took the night shift, Annie had finished reciting him the tale about her two cats just last night. Although those stories were just for his own enjoyment, he was half convinced they were some attempt at a new method of torture and he was test subject number one. He hated this, this feeling of isolation that the world would keep spinning and, no matter what, even once he left the cage, he would still be followed around by his father in one way or another, constantly in some sort of cage. He hated that he had traded a part of his soul for a cage, and not even a glided one at that, he thought, laughing at his own joke, he really was going insane.

"No more grins, Young Princeling" Amelia spoke out in the darkness he lifted his head to see her leaning against the pillar, eyes shining once again with pride in the darkness.

"I am no prince, Amelia, and if youre missing

my beautiful smile you should have said, " Icarus said producing the slyest grin he could muster. "Ah and the lion bares all his teeth, Only 3 more months and then youre free, young princeling, " she said a smile evident in her voice "3 more months and 2 days, actually" Icarus replied not taking the bait with her new favourite endearment. Good to know you are not fixating on anything in particular" Amelia replied starkly. "For your information Amelia I am enjoying my time away from the cloaks and daggers of court life and yes it is nice to sit and think, now did you come here for any particular reason or just to gloat about your access to the sun" Icarus said gazing down at his pale arms. "No I have not come to gloat, as much as you wish it not to be true you were part of the rebellion, you were the sword that ended the tyranny even if it came from your own father" Icarus stood to his full height slamming both hands against the bars of his cell, eyes narrowing at Amelia's "do not speak to me of my father, you have no right to speak of him" Icarus's own anger reflecting back on Amelia. "I have every right to speak of him. He murdered the only family I had left, he ruined your life he was a monster and I am not sorry he's dead" Amelia finished her rant her anger had left her with every she expelled, he felt like a priest being forced to listen to a confession he didn't want to hear. "I am sorry for what happened to your Grandparents I really am But I think we can both agree I don't deserve this cage" Icarus said "Really? You don't think you deserve to be here, yeah Well, I think we can both agree my grandparents did not deserve DEATH!" Amelia screamed from the very pits of her soul. "See you in four months, Young Princeling" "It's only 3 " Icarus contended "Yeah will now it's four!"

With those parting words, Amelia stormed out of the jail kicking the tall oak wardrobe by the door as she went. "As temperamentally as ever, Dearest Amelia "Icarus murmured

once she had left, it had become his favourite hobby to ruffles her feathers, smiling he turned back to his designated thinking corner, but a flash

117

of gold caught his eye, It looked like some sort of mirror that had got dislodged when Amelia had kicked the wardrobe, he was about to dismiss it but realised the background in the mirror didn't match his background "oh god, Amelia. AMELIA¡'. He hadn't seen a picture of the king since before he left for the army "AMELIA!" Before he had hit puberty "AMELIA¡' Fredrickson told him it was a lie, a good one but a lie, this changed everything " AMELIA! I FOUND HIM...I FOUND THE HEIR!"

Printed in Great Britain
by Amazon